12/01

P9-CDB-510

Ishmael

BRITISH TERRITORY

Yellowstone R.

GREAT PLAINS

North Platte River

South Platte River

Missouri River

Mississippi River

Illinois River

Canadian River

Arkansas River

Red River

Rio Grande River

Mississippi River

Wabash River

Ohio River

St. Louis

INDIANA
TERRITORY

MISSISSIPPI
TERRITORY

KY

TN

ME

VT

NH

NY

MA

RI

CT

PA

OH

NJ

MD

ALLEGHENY MOUNTAINS

VA

APPALACHIAN MOUNTAINS

NC

SC

GA

FL

THE UNITED STATES
1803–1840
LOUISIANA PURCHASE

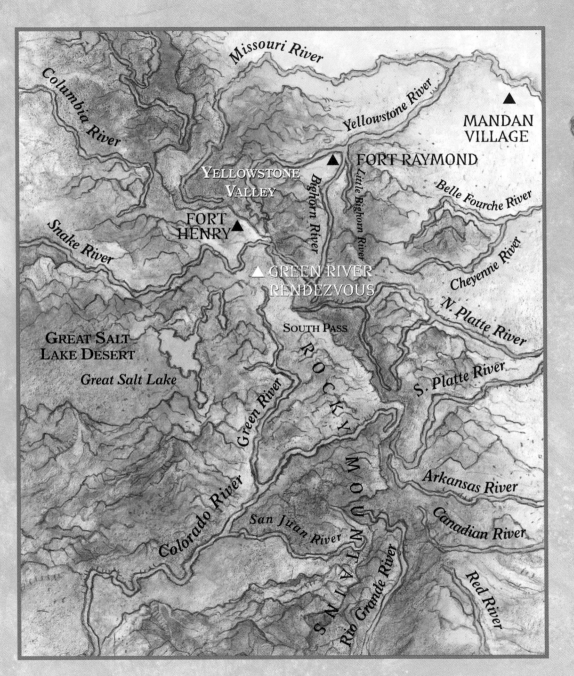

BRITISH TERRITORY

Yellowstone R.

North Platte River

South Platte River

Missouri River

Mississippi River

Illinois River

GREAT PLAINS

Canadian River

Arkansas River

Wabash River

INDIANA
TERRITORY

St. Louis

Mississippi River

Red River

Rio Grande River

KY

TN

MISSISSIPPI
TERRITORY

GA

FL

Ohio River

OH

PA

NY

VT

ME

NH

MA

RI

CT

NJ

MD

VA

ALLEGHENY MOUNTAINS

APPALACHIAN MOUNTAINS

NC

SC

THE UNITED STATES

1803–1840

LOUISIANA PURCHASE

Mountain Men

TRUE GRIT AND TALL TALES

Andrew Glass

A DOUBLEDAY BOOK FOR YOUNG READERS

A Doubleday Book for Young Readers

Published by Random House Children's Books
a division of Random House, Inc.
1540 Broadway, New York, New York 10036

Doubleday and the anchor with dolphin colophon are trademarks of Random House, Inc.

Visit us on the Web! www.randomhouse.com/kids
Educators and librarians, for a variety of teaching tools, visit us at
www.randomhouse.com/teachers

Library of Congress Cataloging-in-Publication Data
Glass, Andrew.
    Mountain men: true grit and tall tales / Andrew Glass.
      p. cm.
    Summary: Describes the lives of the beaver trappers who were the first explorers of the American West beyond the Rocky Mountains, and some of the tall tales that made them legends.
    ISBN 0-385-32555-X (trade)   0-385-90841-5 (lib. bdg.)
    1. Pioneers—West (U.S.) Biography Anecdotes Juvenile literature. 2. West (U.S.)—History—To 1848 Anecdotes Juvenile literature.
    3. West (U.S.) Biography Anecdotes Juvenile literature. 4. Trappers—West (U.S.) Biography Anecdotes Juvenile literature.
    5. Explorers—West (U.S.) Biography Anecdotes Juvenile literature. 6. Frontier and pioneer life—West (U.S.) Anecdotes—Juvenile literature. [1. Trappers. 2. Explorers. 3. West (U.S.)—History—To 1848.] I. Title.
F592.G545 2000
978'.02'0922—dc21
[B]   99-12776
                                             CIP

The text of this book is set in 13-point Italian Old Style.
Book design by Trish P. Watts
Manufactured in the United States of America
June 2001
10 9 8 7 6 5 4 3 2 1

I have sought to picture a fleeting phase of our national life; not omitting its grotesque, lawless features; not concealing my admiration for the adventurous pioneers who have founded great States from the Mississippi to the Pacific, and made new geography for the American Union.

—ALBERT D. RICHARDSON, *Beyond the Mississippi*, 1867

I dedicate this book to Samuel Clemens, who promised never to let dull facts get in the way of telling a true story.

—ANDREW GLASS

THE LOUISIANA PURCHASE

With the Louisiana Purchase of 1803, President Thomas Jefferson more than doubled the size of the United States. Most Americans thought the wily French emperor Napoleon had hoodwinked Jefferson, selling him a savage wilderness of empty prairie and rocky desert unfit for settlement by decent folks.

President Jefferson commissioned Meriwether Lewis and William Clark to explore America's new 827,000 square miles of frontier. On a bright May afternoon in 1804 they set out on their journey with forty-five rugged hunters and woodsmen. The Corps of Discovery, as they were called, followed maps drawn mostly from hearsay and legend. They expected to cross one narrow range of towering mountains leading to a great inland sea. Along the way they hoped to meet the legendary Indian tribe descended from a twelfth-century Prince of Wales. They'd even heard tales of prehistoric woolly mammoths and a mountain of rock salt eighty miles long. The secret purpose of the expedition, however, was to search for a legend—not the lost tribes of Israel, though the explorers were not without hope of finding them too—but the mythical water route to the Pacific Ocean called the Northwest Passage.

All that summer and into the fall the members of Lewis and Clark's expedition struggled up the Missouri River in their twenty-oar keelboat, enduring violent rainstorms, swarms of mosquitoes, snakebites, illness and the death of one of their party from appendicitis. Some sixteen hundred miles upriver in present-day North Dakota, when temperatures dropped to forty-eight degrees below zero, they accepted the hospitality of the Mandan Indians, whom the explorers suspected of speaking Welsh.

Come spring, countless beaver swam alongside their boat as they continued upriver. On May twenty-sixth, near the headwaters of the Missouri, they saw for the first time the dazzling snow-covered peaks of what they called the Shining Mountains. The explorers plodded cross-country toward the new western edge of the United States. They were harassed by fierce grizzly bears. Thickets of cactus tore their feet through their moccasins. Finally they clambered up a sharp ridge at the Continental Divide, expecting to see the wide Columbia River, gateway to the Northwest Passage, flowing peacefully westward down a gradual plain to the sea. Instead they saw range upon range of jagged, snow-covered peaks disappearing far into the distance. By then winter threatened to trap the Corps of Discovery in the desolate wilderness.

From the Shoshone they learned of a steep, rocky trail through the mountains, one regularly used even in winter by Shoshone women and children. The explorers decided to attempt it themselves and were soon hopelessly lost in swirling snow. Starving and unable to find game, they ate their skeletal horses, then the leather soles of their moccasins. Before the explorers were rescued at the western edge of the Bitterroot Range by friendly Nez Percé Indians, who had never before seen white men, they had gobbled up even their last remaining candles.

The Nez Percé helped them to build canoes, and the expedition paddled, hungry and cold, through driving late-winter rain, down the swift current of the Clearwater to the Snake River and into the wide Columbia. As the miserable fog lifted on November 7, 1805, the Corps of Discovery glimpsed, at long last, the Pacific Ocean. They made camp at the mouth of the Columbia, on the south bank. On a pine tree by the sea, William Clark carved

William Clark, December 3rd, 1805.
By Land. From the U States.

It was August 12, 1806, before the Corps of Discovery—half starved, ragged and exhausted—returned to its first wintering place with the Mandan Indians along the Missouri River. The explorers were still a long way from St. Louis, but the worst was finally behind them. Captain Lewis sat on a soft beaver pelt (along the way a hungry fiddle player had mistaken Lewis's ragged rawhide britches for the back end of an elk and shot him). He dreamed of a hot bath and a sumptuous hotel dinner served on spotless china plates.

So Captain Lewis could scarcely believe his ears when Private John Colter, who had endured the nearly nine thousand miles of shivering cold, mortal fear and hunger, asked to be released from military service so that he might return upriver to try his luck in the fur trade as a trapper. Permission was granted, and John Colter paddled back up the Missouri into the lonely wilderness. To survive, he learned the wilderness skills of the Indians. He called the Rocky Mountains his home, and created the legend of the first American mountain man.

THE FUR TRADE

Europeans had long considered the soft pelts of beaver, mink, otter and marten the only natural resource worth mentioning on the entire savage North American continent. By the early 1800s, when tall beaver hats became the rage among the gentry in Boston and New York, the eastern states were already nearly trapped out. So John Jacob Astor's American Fur Company established an outpost along the Columbia River, where beaver were still plentiful. In 1807 Manuel Lisa, a St. Louis merchant, built the first American trading post, Fort Raymond, at the junction of the Yellowstone and Bighorn rivers. In 1822 Captain William H. Ashley and Major Andrew Henry placed a notice in the St. Louis *Republican* for their new Rocky Mountain Fur Company with the idea of outfitting independent trappers:

> **Enterprising Young Men,**
> **willing to ascend the**
> **Missouri to its source . . .**

Unlike trappers hired at a fixed salary, free trappers sold their beaver pelts to the highest bidder. Wandering alone or in twos and threes, they blazed trails through the dangerous mountain passes deep into hostile Indian country in search of "hairy banknotes."

The lonely trapper waded chest deep through icy creeks, fearing to make the slightest careless noise. He set traps below the water's surface, baiting them with a musky beaver secretion called medicine, and returned in the biting cold before dawn to collect the "gone beavers." He skinned his catch on the spot, then stretched each pelt on a willow hoop. Once it was dry he folded it with others into plews, wrapped them carefully and buried his cache. A full-grown beaver weighed from thirty to sixty pounds. An average pelt weighed about two pounds and was worth as much as eighteen dollars. A good trapper might carry out a thousand or even two thousand dollars' worth of pelts, while back East, skilled workers toiled in dungeonlike factories for a dollar and a half a day.

Come mid-June (a mountain man marked the passing days by knotting a string), he dug up his cache of plews, loaded down his ponies and rode to rendezvous. At rendezvous trappers sold their hairy banknotes to the company traders, and with their hard-earned cash they bought everything from knives to pickles and cheap jewelry and calico for their Indian wives at inflated company prices. The company in turn resold the plews for a huge profit in St. Louis.

After the first rendezvous at Henry's Fork on the Green River in 1825, hundreds of mountain men arrived every summer, along with thousands of Indians (often mortal enemies back in the high country). Across their saddles they carried Hawkin rifles, said to be accurate at two hundred yards and packing enough of a wallop to bring down a grizzly. They held bragging contests, lying contests, shooting contests, knife-throwing contests, races and wrestling bouts that often deteriorated into outright brawls, as they gambled away their hard-earned money. "There goes hos and beaver" meant losing everything. By the time most trappers returned to the wilderness, they'd lost all but their traps and the overpriced powder and lead they'd bought from the company traders,

and maybe a frying pan, a little coffee for their coffeepot, some salt and a tightly woven Indian blanket. Still, they'd never had to leave the wilderness, and that was just the way they liked it. Only greenhorn porkeaters depended on civilized fixin's.

Death was always near at hand. Trappers regularly drowned; died of smallpox, hydrophobia, rattlesnake bites or falls; were buried in snow slides; or simply starved or froze to death in the deep snow. They might be mauled by grizzlies or killed by Indians or their own roughneck comrades. They also got sick and expired of dysentery, thanks to eating nothing but fat meat. Gunshot and arrow wounds were of course commonplace. According to an old mountain man named Ohio Pattie, 116 of his friends rode into the mountains in 1826, but only 16 rode out again. It was said of the legendary mountain men that fear found within their hearts no resting place.

Quaker Hat

Stovepipe Hat

Tricorn Hat

Lady's Bonnet

THE LEGENDARY MOUNTAIN MEN

Mountain men were always the heroes of their own tall tales because each storyteller reckoned he was the equal of any man alive. They dressed for their role as a new breed of American hero in buckskin leggings, jackets with long fringes called whangs (useful for emergency mending), moccasins and fur or warm wool hats decorated with porcupine quills, Indian style. Over one shoulder hung a strap holding a powder horn and a bullet pouch for balls and flints. They tucked a butcher knife into their belt, along with a tomahawk. A dried deerskin overshirt served as armor for deflecting arrows.

When the days grew dark and the streams froze over, the beaver hibernated in their lodges. Mountain men sought out a sheltered hollow with enough cottonwood boughs to feed their mules. There they holed up until spring. They stowed their packs and saddles under arched frameworks of bent saplings covered with stretched skins, and lined their cozy shelters with warm buffalo robes. Antlers served as hooks for clothes and for drying meat.

Cabin fever could be the death of even the orneriest old hos. So they eased the boredom of being cooped up together for the long, cold winter months by telling stories. They entertained each other with a remarkable blend of Indian legends and fantastical tales of their own harrowing escapes and adventures.

Mountain men proudly claimed to be the inventors of the American tall tale. Mother Nature, they said, stretched the truth taller and wider in the Rocky Mountains, just naturally making grand liars out of ordinary frontier yarn spinners. But these masters of exaggeration, like Jim Bridger, and gaudy liars, like Jim Beckwourth, were said to know the twists and turns of every creek bed and the whereabouts of every badger hole and beaver dam from the wide Missouri to the Central Rockies and on down to Mexico.

John Colter

*Mountain men have little fear of God
and none at all of the devil, so they say.*

After trapping with two companions for a season, John Colter set out alone in 1807 to search for beaver and also for Indian tribes who might be well disposed to fur traders. He followed Indian trails into the valley of the Yellowstone, up the Bighorn and Wind rivers and west to the Snake River. He returned to Fort Raymond with tales of boiling sulfurous springs, geysers and smoking mud holes he'd seen with his own eyes in the Yellowstone Valley. Nobody believed him, though. They thought he'd been robbed of his reason by the spirits of the woods.

COLTER'S RUN

Mountain men lazing around a campfire enjoyed nothing as much as a good brag about how some ol' hos managed to keep his scalp. This tale of the West's most celebrated footrace was one of many yarns about narrow escapes.

In 1808, near the Jefferson Fork at the headwaters of the Missouri, John Colter and his partner, John Potts, were checking their traps. When Potts saw a party of Blackfoot warriors nearly upon them, he instinctively grabbed his rifle and was promptly punctured by so many Blackfoot arrows, shot from both sides of the creek, that he died looking like a porcupine. The warriors took the cooler-headed Colter prisoner, stripped him jaybird naked and taunted him. "How would you like to die?" asked a Blackfoot chief, poking him in the ribs.

"Please, sir," John begged (mountain men spoke the languages of many tribes and could communicate in signs with most others), "stomp me, bury me alive and lift my hair or tie me to a buffalo's tail, but please, please, please don't ask me to race. Skin me alive if you must. Stake me out and leave me to be nibbled bit by bit into the next world by red ants and foul-breathed coyotes. But please don't make fun of my sad skinny legs by chasing me across the prairie under the hot sun. I am slow as a turtle and it would make sorry sport." His piteous pleading sealed his fate. The Indians decided they'd give their captive a head start in a race for his life. The warriors doubled over with laughter at their murderous joke as their captive limped away on wobbly legs.

But when they saw John take to his heels like a jackrabbit, dancing painfully over prickly pears, they realized at once they'd been tricked. He sprinted so fast a blood vessel burst in his nose. John soon left the hundreds of enraged Blackfoot warriors so far behind that they were nothing but angry shouts on the wind—all but one dogged pursuer. Realizing he couldn't outrun his fleet-footed enemy, John suddenly whirled

and confronted him. The sight of the naked mountain man, stained with his own bright red blood in the pink sunset, knocked the last breath out of the nearly winded Blackfoot warrior. He stumbled and collapsed from weariness and fright. John Colter dove into the freezing Jefferson River.

Hiding beneath a beaver lodge, he watched the angry Indians searching for him. And when night fell, he escaped by swimming five miles downstream in the dark. Finally dragging himself up the riverbank, naked and unarmed, the first rugged mountain man did the only thing left to do. He started walking. Seven days later he arrived blistered, torn and bloody, at Fort Raymond, some three hundred miles away at the mouth of the Bighorn River, having eaten nothing on the way but breadroot.

———◆———

It wasn't long before John Colter had another deadly encounter with the Blackfoot. This time he promised he'd leave the Shining Mountains forever—"Day after tomorrow!"—if the Good Lord would just spare his life one more time. True to his word, in 1810, with none of his trapping companions left alive to join him, John Colter leapt into a buffalo-skin canoe and paddled two thousand miles to St. Louis. He wasn't a mapmaker and he hadn't kept a journal, so no one except his old commander, William Clark, believed him when he described the sulfurous, bubbling mud of the Yellowstone Valley: "I've seen the place where Hell bubbles up." John Colter died in 1813 in St. Louis.

What did the Blackfoot Indians, so named because they colored their moccasins with ashes, have against the mountain men, anyway? The story goes that Meriwether Lewis killed two young Blackfoot to prevent them from stealing the Corps of Discovery's precious horses and provisions. The Blackfoot, however, saw the killings differently and swore an oath of revenge against all who followed.

Jedediah Strong Smith

WITH A BIBLE AND A RIFLE

Jedediah Strong Smith, a devout Methodist, read both official volumes about Lewis and Clark's expedition. He also prayed for guidance before he signed on with Captain Ashley in 1822 to lead a band of rowdy farm boys and tough river men up the Missouri to its source. They were inexperienced trappers, terrified of the trackless Rocky Mountain wilderness. So they put up with Bible-toting Jedediah's danged piety because he was an extraordinary woodsman.

Grizzlies were another dreaded enemy of the mountain men. One old mountain man swore he counted two hundred grizzlies in a single day. They ruled the West like giant mountain trolls, inspiring tall tales and true accounts and a gruesome mixture of both.

In 1823 Jed Smith was searching for a way to avoid hostile Indians by making the first overland trek west of the Missouri into Yellowstone country through the Black Hills. One day he was charged by a giant grizzly. It grasped Jed's whole head in its gaping jaws, picked him up and slammed him to the earth so hard his ribs cracked. His face was mauled and his right ear nearly torn off.

"Stitch me up!" he shouted at young Jon Clyman. But all the boy could find was coarse thread for repairing moccasins. "Mend me the best you can, son," Jed ordered. When the boy lamented that the mangled ear was beyond fixing, Jed replied, "You must try some way or other." Jon sewed round and round through the torn skin. Miraculously Jed survived and the ear healed. He was back on the trail within days. But after that he let his hair grow long on one side.

"Let this be a lesson to you on the character of grizzlies," he said.

Determined to blaze new trails, learn all he could of the wilderness and make his fortune at fur trapping, Jedediah Smith explored more of the West than anyone before him. Riding south of the Sweetwater River in 1824, he was directed by the Crow and Cheyenne to a treeless valley. This windswept mountain gateway to the Oregon Trail came to be called the South Pass. In 1826 he was the first American to travel overland, across the Rocky Mountains, to California.

By 1830 Smith held the trapper's record of 668 pelts in a single season and returned to St. Louis, wealthy enough to devote himself to his journals and maps. He was just thirty-two years old when he made one more trip west across the Cimarron Desert to Santa Fe. While scouting for water to rescue his fellow travelers, he was killed by Comanche, who left his body for the coyotes. His journals and charts were never completed, so others took credit for discovering the territories he'd explored.

Hugh Glass

A Tough Old Mountain Man

Wherever mountain men settled back under the shelter of drafty buffalo tents on freezing winter nights, someone was sure to tell the tale of Hugh Glass. His was a story of how grit and pure orneriness can overcome the meanness of grizzlies and the mean-spiritedness of men as well as the hardships of the wilderness.

Hugh Glass joined a trapping expedition in 1823, venturing with Major Henry up the Yellowstone River. The Arikara were on the warpath, so Major Henry ordered the men to stay together. But old Hugh, never much for taking orders, wandered off in search of something to shoot for supper. Hearing terrible howls and screams, the others crashed through the brush to find a grizzly tearing at the old mountain man with sharp teeth and claws. They fired their rifles and the bear ran off roaring, leaving Hugh torn up and gasping for breath through a wide gash in his throat.

Though someone sewed the old man back together, there was little hope. They waited politely through the night for him to die. Come morning Hugh was still breathing in shallow gasps and snorts. Major Henry declared it wasn't fair to risk the scalps of the whole troop by staying with Hugh.

"Someone must stay behind and wait for Hugh to go to his reward," the major declared. Young Jim Bridger stepped forward. Hoping to sound as brave as his hero, Jedediah Smith, he said, "Heck, I'll stay." But Jim was too green to stay behind alone. No experienced woodsman volunteered until Major Henry offered a reward. For forty bucks—dollars were called bucks because back East the skin of a male deer was worth a dollar—John Fitzgerald agreed to keep young Jim company until the dying old trapper drew his last breath.

"Bury him proper, then hurry along and catch up," ordered Major Henry.

No sooner had the crew moved on than Fitzgerald started badgering the boy. "Old Hugh is good as gone under anyway," he said. Yet Jim went on nursing the old man, moistening his feverish lips with creek water and brushing the flies off him. Exasperated after five days of waiting, Fitzgerald suggested putting Hugh out of his misery. Jim agreed it would be for the best, but neither had the stomach for it. Finally, on the sixth day, the boy was convinced there was nothing to do but move on. "We've already lingered overlong for our own good, and the old buzzard's as good as dead anyhow," said Fitzgerald. When they left they took everything. "There's no sense in leaving a rifle with a man who's as good as dead, nor a serviceable butcher knife neither."

Stealthily they made their way north along the Yellowstone River and rejoined the crew. They told Major Henry they'd buried old Hugh where he'd died and marked the grave with a stone. Everyone agreed Hugh Glass had been a tough old mountain man right to the end. Jim shamefully took his share of the reward. Otherwise someone might suspect he'd run off the faithless way he had.

Back in the woods, Old Hugh finally opened his eyes. "I must be dead," he thought, "elsewise there ain't no explanation for why I've been left behind all alone." After a spell he began remembering what had happened in bits and snatches: the sharp teeth, the blood. "Forty-dollar reward," he seemed to recall, and "Old buzzard's good as dead." Risking opening his wounds again, he rolled painfully down to where a spring ran under a thicket. He lived for some days on pure rage and chokecherries, pondering the shameful perfidy of leaving a companion helpless in the wilderness. Some say the old man ate a rattlesnake, swallowing it in small bites, and the meanness in it gave him strength enough to begin crawling upriver.

Most likely he would have starved along the way but for gorging himself on the carcass of a buffalo calf brought down by a wolf pack. The next day he staggered from sunup to sundown, dreaming of revenge with every feeble step. Two hundred miles later, the soldiers at Fort Kiowa saw something that seemed scarcely human. He shuffled up to the stockade muttering to himself, "Commencing with their ears, I'll slice clear to their noses and keep right on carving down to their toes."

Within weeks the wiry old mountain man rode back out the gate, toward the high country of the upper Missouri River. He carried a borrowed rifle and a brand-new butcher knife he'd bought special to cut off the ears of Jim Bridger and John Fitzgerald.

He caught up with Jim at Fort Henry. The boy believed he was seeing old Hugh's mutilated ghost come to haunt him in revenge for his unfaithfulness. He cried out and apologized to the hideous apparition. His sincerity melted the old man's grizzled heart. "I reckon a porkeater such as yourself is jest too green to know any better," he said. Jim was ashamed, but relieved to be freed from his burdensome lie. Through burning tears he swore that he would never again be false to his word, nor abandon a partner no matter what.

As for John Fitzgerald, some say the Arikara killed him and took his hair before Hugh could settle the score. Others say he joined the army to save himself from the old man's wrath. Still others insist old Hugh met up with Fitzgerald at Council Bluffs and hoisted him up by the throat, intending to spill his guts with the gleaming butcher knife he'd bought special for the occasion. There wasn't a trapper in the crew foolhardy enough to place himself betwixt the fury of the old mountain man and his revenge. But old Hugh Glass surprised them all that day, and himself too if the truth be known. Loud as the big ol' grizzly that had laid him low, he roared, "Settle the matter with your own conscience and your God. But give me back my rifle!"

In the winter of 1832, the Blackfoot ambushed old Hugh Glass on the frozen Missouri River and took his life. Jim Bridger became widely known as the most faithful and honorable leader of mountain men. His deeds were always as good as his word.

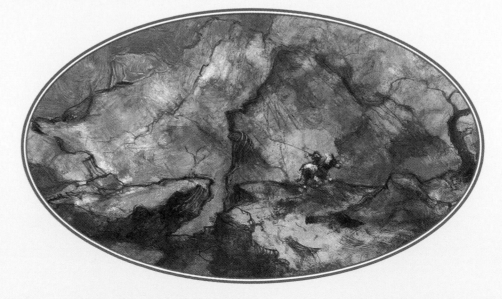

Jim Bridger

KING OF THE MOUNTAIN MEN

One of the first to sign on with Major Henry was an eighteen-year-old blacksmith's apprentice named Jim Bridger. Someone must have read Jim the advertisement in the St. Louis paper, because the boy was said to be "perfectly ignorant of all knowledge contained in books." He couldn't even read his own name, but he could make an accurate map of any region he'd ever passed through. He spoke French, Spanish and the languages of many tribes. Besides being a trapper, he was an explorer. On a bet in 1825 as to the course of the Bear River, just west of the present-day Wyoming border, he ran the rapids in a buffalo-skin boat. When he bobbed into a vast expanse of salt water, his first guess was that he'd reached the wide Pacific Ocean. But he returned and announced his discovery of the Great Salt Lake.

Ol' Gabe, as his friends called him, became one of America's all-time great inventors of tall tales. He described powerful geysers, spouting seventy feet high with the regularity of gentlemen's timepieces, "hissing something terrific." He claimed to have seen a river that flowed some fifteen miles downhill from a huge mountain lake, through a deep canyon, to springs hot enough for cooking. Then it descended farther, until it collected in pools just perfect for warm baths, near a cave of vermilion that warriors used to paint themselves red. Jim was only recounting the wonders of the Yellowstone Valley he'd seen with his own eyes. But folks responded, just as they had to John Colter's accounts of Yellowstone's natural wonders, "That's preposterous!" Jim grew so vexed and aggravated with the injustice of it all that he came to tell his tale of Yellowstone's obsidian cliffs this way:

"While hunting one day, I happened upon a fine elk, the likes of which I'd never in my life laid eyes on before. So naturally I raised my rifle and fired, kaboom!!!! I'm not accustomed to missing, but there's a first time for everything, so I reloaded and fired again. The handsome elk, not even affrighted by the noise, went right on grazing. So I crept closer, reloaded and fired once more. Again my most earnest attempt didn't even ruffle his fur. Well sir, if'n I couldn't shoot him, due to some altitudinous peculiarity of nature, I resolved to club the danged buck to death. Swinging my rifle by the barrel, I rushed forward and collided headlong with an invisible wall, nearly knocking myself senseless, and causing a considerable ringing in my ears like church bells.

"When I recovered my senses I saw that the magnificent buck elk was still grazing peacefully. I concluded that I had collided with a glass mountain, and a natural telescope to boot. The buck looked to be just a few yards off, but I reckoned it to be nearly twenty-five miles away."

Such tall tales became known as Jim Bridger's Lies.

Another favorite tale of Jim's went like this:

"One evening near sundown, after long months on my own, I rode my sleepy horse in the direction of a familiar campsite. I was riding through a region of petrified wood when I realized I was near up onto the edge of a calamitous deep chasm.

"Looking forward as I was to pleasant company and yarn spinning around a campfire and being so long in the saddle without rest, I considered the notion of jumping across. But thinking better of it, I scanned the horizon for a possible means of riding around. Meanwhile my horse had plumb fallen asleep. He continued clippity-clopping right along with his eyes closed.

"As we neared the precipice I shouted 'Whoa!' In my frantic desperation I hardly noticed that we had clip-clopped right off the edge of the cliff! I looked down my nose into the bottomless canyon and I sat perfectly still, fearing to jostle the natural forces. When we arrived at the other side I scratched my head some, and more than that I can't tell ya. Except gravity ain't no sure thing in my experience!"

Jim Bridger often told the tale of being chased right to the edge of a similar precipice by a band of Blackfoot.

"Every time I turned in my saddle I shot one, reloaded and shot another and another. By the time I got to the edge there weren't but one left. Ol' Goliath himself couldn'ta been any bigger than this feller, and he was plenty sore. We went at it tooth and claw until he grabbed me by the hair and dangled me over the edge of the cliff."

At this point in his story, Jim would hesitate, appearing distracted, as if he'd lost his train of thought, until some greenhorn demanded impatiently, "Well, what happened?"

Then Jim Bridger, the king of the mountain men, would reply simply, "I got kilt!"

———◆———

After 1840 Jim became a guide to settlers and an army scout, founding Fort Bridger on the Oregon Trail in 1843 and blazing the Overland Trail. He opened the West to thousands of settlers' wagons. On a piece of wrapping paper with a chunk of charcoal from a campfire, Jim drew a route for the Union Pacific Railroad through the Rocky Mountains. The coming of trains brought to an end the true wilderness of the mountain men. Jim Bridger died in 1881.

Mike Fink

A RING-TAILED ROARER

By the time Mike Fink signed on with the Missouri Fur Company in 1823, he was already a legend as the King of the Keelboatmen. The story goes that the day Mike was born he refused mother's milk and hollered for a bottle of rye whiskey. Mike claimed he could "outrun, outjump, outshoot, outbrag, outdrink and outfight, no holds barred, any man on both sides of the Mississippi." Mike Fink always wore a red feather in his cap. He was the best shot in Pittsburgh, so they say, with his Kentucky rifle named Bang-All.

Powerful keelboatmen pushed seventy-foot keelboats upstream using long poles against the strong river current. When steam-powered boats took over the hauling of goods on the Mississippi in 1815, gentlemanly riverboat life left no place for ring-tailed roarers like Mike. Townsfolk didn't welcome the ferocious keelboatmen either.

Even Mike Fink couldn't ignore civilization when the long arm of law and order finally came to the river. In Westport, Indiana, one afternoon, so the story goes, while Mike was telling one of his scrapping, cheating, stealing, bullying and shooting for no good reason yarns, he noticed a little old man, who looked bored. Mike didn't give a hoot what civilized folks might say about him as long as they didn't say he told a dull tale.

"I can't abide a man who's as glum as a dead catfish," Mike shouted.

"Is that so?" replied the little sourpuss.

"If'n ya force me to," roared Mike, "I'll beat a sense of humor inta ya."

"Is that so?"

"Calamity's a-comin'!" Mike shouted, exasperated and fixing to rattle the old man's yellow teeth loose. But the sour little man turned into a whirling cyclone of flying fists and kicking feet. He sent Mike sprawling.

Mike Fink stood and puffed himself up. "I'm a ring-tailed roarer, half wild horse and half cockeyed alligator," he yelled. He took a mighty swing only to get kicked hard in the stomach for his trouble. "I'm Ol' Snag," he gasped. "I got the prettiest wife, the sharpest shooting iron and the ugliest dog in all creation." He rushed at the little fellow, only to fall back again. Four times more he tried to grab hold, till he was plumb out of breath and out of brag too. "Mister, I jest can't do nuthin' with ya. You're tougher to chaw than buckskin."

"I'm the sheriff in these parts, and I'll lock up the mess of you river men if you're not outa town in ten minutes."

"Five's plenty," said Mike.

"Is that so?"

The Rocky Mountain wilderness was the only place left uncivilized enough for Mike Fink. At the age of fifty-two he signed on with Andrew Henry. Other washed-up river men and ordinary roughneck farm boys were transformed by the wilderness into mountain men, but Mike's legendary orneriness got him killed within the year.

Mike had a young admirer and companion named Carpenter. Mike claimed to have raised the boy from a cub. They say he was of no better character than Mike himself and nearly as good a shot. The two friends planned to hole up that first winter at Fort Henry. To amuse themselves they challenged other trappers to a nerve-racking contest called "shooting the tin cup," taking turns shooting cups of whiskey off each other's heads at thirty paces. The point of the game was to spill the whiskey without shooting your opponent. Naturally they had few takers, so they grew fond of getting liquored up and performing the feat themselves. Roaring with laughter, they washed their hair with spilled tangle root whiskey.

Finally fed up with their drunken deviltry, Major Henry said they were just too cussed mean even for the company of roughneck Rocky Mountain fur trappers. "You're not even fit for uncivilized society!" he declared. Mike responded by calling Fort Henry a skunk hole and walked out, arm in arm with his young friend, to winter in a cave nearby.

No one knows how it is they fell out during the long winter months together. A first-class case of cabin fever, folks said. But by spring the two were barely on speaking terms. When Mike suggested they celebrate the first thaw by shooting the tin cup for old times' sake, Carpenter was suspicious. He took careful aim and knocked the cup from Mike's head, but the shot grazed Mike's scalp.

"That ain't the way I taught ya," Mike growled. He cocked Bang-All. "Hold your noddle steady, boy, and don't spill the whiskey!" he said, and fired. The young man fell dead without a groan. "Carpenter," said Mike, "you've spilt the whiskey."

No one could prove he'd done it on purpose, and some said he was truly miserable at the loss of his friend. But a man named Talbot, the gunsmith at Fort Henry, called Mike a cold-blooded murderer. The way some folks tell it, Talbot overheard Mike bragging as to how he'd shot the boy on purpose and was glad to see him dead. So Talbot took revenge directly, shooting Mike with Carpenter's own gun. Or it could be that Talbot's fear of the tough old river man got the best of him and he shot Mike just because he was scared. Either way Mike Fink's bullying nature finally got him killed.

Mike was one of the wildest men in all the untamed West and a popular legend in his day. But tastes have changed and he's no longer mentioned much as a frontier hero. Still, it must be said that he was a gifted liar. Mike Fink had the prettiest wife, the sharpest shooting iron and the ugliest dog.

Is that so?

Kit Carson

FIVE FOOT TWO AND COUGAR ALL THE WAY

Christopher (Kit) Carson wasn't even a passable liar. He didn't talk much in general. When he spoke, he spoke softly. But there were plenty of stories told about him. Kit Carson was the most famous mountain man of all.

At the rendezvous of 1835 in the Green River Valley, a bone-crunching, eye-gouging French Canadian trapper named Shunar swaggered around insulting both Indians and trappers. He was as big as a grizzly and nearly as mean. Even scrappy trappers and fearless Indians, who never in their lives ran from a fight, walked a wide circle to keep out of his way. One evening around the campfire Shunar got to boasting and bellowing. "Lily-livered Americans hadn't ought to be in the mountains at all," he said. "They's all porkeaters and ain't near tough enough for the trapper's life. Proof is that there ain't a one of 'em ain't skeert of me."

Kit spoke up softly. "I ain't skeert."

The bully looked down at the little trapper. "I'd thrash a full-growed man if'n he spoke up to me that way," he growled. "But for a little bitty morsel of a fella like you, I reckon I'll just cut a switch and paddle you till you're tender enough to eat for dinner."

Kit looked up at the big Canadian. "Mind your manners," he said, "or I'll rip your guts out right through your nose."

Duels were an ordinary occurrence at rendezvous. Hot-tempered backwoodsmen were often a danger to each other, particularly when under the influence of rotgut whiskey. The Canadian grabbed his rifle, leapt onto his big horse and rode off a ways. "I'm gonna rub you out, half-pint!" he threatened. Kit mounted up too, looking hot enough to sizzle spit. The bully whirled around and the two rushed at each other like knights of old. Shunar leveled his rifle and rode in close. But Kit's courageous pony was trained to throw itself against a running buffalo. At the last moment it crashed into the Canadian's oversized horse. Shunar's aim was ruined. His shot lopped off a lock of Kit's hair. Quick as a spark, Kit winged him with his pistol.

The big bully slunk away to tend his badly wounded arm, promising not to cause any more trouble. But Kit Carson was still aggravated. "I can't abide a bully," he muttered. "But I hadn't ought to have lost my temper. Hot tempers and gun-play can't shine with me."

———◆———

Christopher Houston Carson was born in Kentucky on Christmas Eve of 1809. At sixteen he ran away from the saddler's shop where he'd been apprenticed. He joined up with a traders' caravan going to Santa Fe in Mexican territory. As soon as he could outfit himself he headed into the mountains, and he wandered the far West as a free trapper for fif-

teen years. He learned everything there was to know about the wilderness and the languages and beliefs of the people who lived there. By the 1830s he was one of the most efficient trappers from Mexico to the Snake River. He could manage a good season even in dangerous Blackfoot country, where others wouldn't leave camp for fear of being shot.

Kit fell in love with an Arapaho woman named Waanibe. According to Kit the Arapaho were a gentle tribe, much concerned with courtesy, who should never be treated roughly. It was said Waanibe (Kit called her Alice) was being tormented by the giant Shunar at the rendezvous of 1835. Kit may have challenged the bully to satisfy the offended Indians, who threatened to turn the trading party into a war party. When Waanibe died, leaving him to care for two daughters, he mar-

ried a Cheyenne woman. Both tribes held him in high esteem.

Kit was the official guide to Frémont's three surveying and mapping explorations from 1842 to 1846. He was given the rank of general in the army and he played a large part in defeating the Indians, opening up for settlers the places he had once loved for their wildness. Later, he became one of the few Indian agents who was trusted by the tribes he'd once fought. He protected them as best he could from government corruption and stupidity. Kit, known to the Indians as the Little Chief, died in 1868. Dozens of dime novels were published about him with titles like *Perils of the Frontier* and *The Fighting Trapper*. But Kit never read one, because he was the only general in the history of the American army who could neither read nor write.

Jim Beckwourth

You cannot pay a free trapper a greater compliment than to mistake him for an Indian.

—WASHINGTON IRVING

When Jim Beckwourth was adopted by the Crow people his life was changed forever. Young trappers—African Americans, Canadians, Scotsmen, Spanish-speaking Mexicans and frontiersmen from the Eastern mountains— would not have survived long in the West without the help of Indians. Many enjoyed tribal protection by marrying into the tribe. Missionaries generally condemned these men as no better than savages, and Jim took plenty of ribbing about "going savage." He later wrote, "Some of the very worst savages I ever saw in the Rocky Mountains were white men."

Jim was often said to be the child of a slave and Sir Jennings Beckwourth, an English planter, who set his handsome son free in St. Louis to make his way in the world. In fact, Jim seems to have been the son of a white working man and a black woman, perhaps a slave, who moved west when Jim was still a boy. Jim hired on as a blacksmith to one of Captain Ashley's first expeditions up the Missouri in 1823.

One evening around the campfire a fellow trapper entertained a band of Crow with a whopper about how Jim himself was one of their tribe, stolen in childhood by the Cheyenne and sold to settlers back East. They all had a good laugh at the tall tale and forgot the whole thing. Some weeks later, Jim was taken prisoner while checking his traps. He was led under guard to the Crow village, where an old woman had heard the story of a stolen boy who had recently returned to the mountains. She looked Jim up and down. To his astonishment she announced that he was her long-lost son.

Jim, renamed Antelope, decided to humor her and live among the Crow just so he could trap beaver in their streams. He led a band called the Dog Warriors, defeating the Blackfoot and Cheyenne in gruesome battles. He later recounted a clash atop a natural rock basin. "Blackfoot blood intermingled with Crow to fill the wide stone bowl," he said. Jim claimed that before leading his Dog Warriors into battle, shouting "Hoo-ki-hi" and waving his tomahawk, he needed his scalping knife to cut away pieces of his clothing and free himself from the adoring grip of his seven wives. Jim Beckwourth was widely admired as one of the finest and gaudiest of liars.

Jim's Indian names were Antelope, Enemy of Horses, Bloody Arm and Medicine Calf. He took many scalps and earned many coups (a warrior's way of keeping an honorable score in battle). The death of a warrior was one coup, the death of two was two coups. Taking a battle-ax or gun also counted as one coup. Though Jim tried to turn his tribe's attention to profitable trapping rather than war, they found horses and honor too great a temptation. "Our enemies steal our horses so we must steal them back," his Dog Warriors told him.

In his autobiography, dictated to T. D. Bonner in 1856, Beckwourth remembered with particular admiration the warrior who always fought by his side, "endowed with extraordinary muscular strength, with the activity of a cat and the speed of an antelope, who always rode the fleetest horse into battle, and was as skillful with weapons as any brave." And yet, he wrote, every day she grew more lovely. Pine Leaf (Bar-chee-am-pe) had sworn to avenge the death of her twin brother, killed by the Cheyenne in his twelfth year. She pledged the Great Spirit never to marry until one hundred of the enemy died by her own hand. Jim was enchanted by her beauty. "Knowing that as a woman she could never be inducted into the secrets of the warrior made her eyes burn like embers," he wrote. "Marry me," he asked.

"If I marry, the Great Spirit, who sees and knows all things, will deny me my revenge," she replied. "Besides, you have too many wives already." But Jim persisted. Even riding into battle he begged, insisting that his strong medicine as war chief demanded it.

"I will be your wife when the pine leaves turn yellow," she promised. Jim galloped giddily into battle, confident that come autumn he would marry Bar-chee-am-pe. When the battle ended it occurred to him that pine leaves never turn yellow. She laughed. "Don't fret so, Enemy of Horses. I will surely marry you when you find a red-haired Indian."

To accommodate their horses' need for fresh grass, Jim's band moved to Clark's Fork off the Yellowstone River. There they took a great encampment of Blackfoot by surprise. In the battle three weasel tails were shot from Jim's eagle-feathered headdress. Pine Leaf won many coups and saved Jim by killing a powerful Blackfoot set on splintering his skull with his battle-ax. When she offered Jim one of her prisoners as a wife, he insisted, "I want no more wives until I've taken to wife the heroine of the Crow."

"Then you must have found a red-haired Indian," she replied.

When the old chief, A-ra-poo-ash, heard the Great Spirit call in a voice like the moaning of the night, he named Jim to succeed him as first counselor and great chief. But the savagery of constant warfare was wearing Jim down. "To gratify a youthful search for adventure," he wrote, "I had traveled the vastness of the Rocky Mountains in summer heats and winter frosts. I had encountered savage beasts and wild men until my deliverance was a prevailing miracle. I had dyed my hand crimson with blood and what had I to show for such a catalog of ruthless deeds?"

As great chief, Jim encouraged the Crow to heed the legend of a once mighty tribe that had been made weak by endless wars. "Turn your battle-axes into beaver traps and your lances into hunting knives," he said. Wealth enough to buy firearms, he told them, would secure the Crow against attack. Besides, as first counselor, Jim was well paid by the American Fur Company to maintain good relations with Indians.

Pine Leaf finally announced, "If I marry any man, I'll marry Medicine Calf" (Jim's new name as first counselor). But Jim realized that death was the only retirement for a war chief. In 1838, after fourteen years in the mountains, he returned to St. Louis, reluctantly abandoning his adopted people.

Jim returned to the wilderness for the last time in 1866, on a mission for the U.S. government to make peace with the tribes along the Powder River in Wyoming, who had risen against pioneers attempting to settle on their land. There the Crow people prepared a great banquet of dog in his honor and poisoned him. They claimed it was the only way to keep their great chief among them forever.

"If I chose to become an Indian," Jim once said, "it concerned no person but myself. By doing so I saved more life and property than a whole regiment of United States regulars could have done."

THE END OF AN ERA

In the late 1830s fur hats went out of fashion, replaced by silk from the China trade. The price of beaver pelts plummeted. "Such a heap of fat meat was not going to shine much longer." That was trapper talk, meaning the life of the free trapper was too good to last. The last rendezvous was held in 1840. Some mountain men became guides for the settlers who were at last venturing onto the plains in wagon trains. Others, like Kit Carson, worked as army scouts and Indian fighters or guided government explorations. Some had made fortunes and returned to civilization with or without their Indian wives and families. Joe Meek, who claimed that when he first went into the high country, Mount Hood was still a hole in the ground, had married a Shoshone (together they raised eight children) and served as U.S. Marshal of the Oregon Territory. Some of the old mountain men vanished forever into the fast-disappearing wilderness, but their tall tales and the stories of their adventures became part of the folklore of the untamed American West.

Mountain Man Necessaries

Newhouse beaver trap—*Trapped the animal between snapping steel jaws.*

Skin boat—*Also called bull boat, it was made of stretched buffalo hide.*

Cache bundle—*Skins, wrapped tightly, were often buried to be retrieved later.*

Hunting knife—*An all-purpose tool, eight to fifteen inches long. An Arkansas Toothpick, as the bowie knife was called, was often a mountain man's only eating implement.*

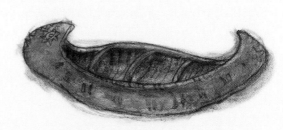

Birchbark canoe—*Sewn together and sealed with pine pitch, it was light enough to be carried when necessary.*

Willow hoop—*Used to stretch scraped and salted beaver skins, it was set in the sun for a day or two.*

Hawkin rifle—*Had a range of 350 yards and was the favorite of mountain men like Jim Bridger.*

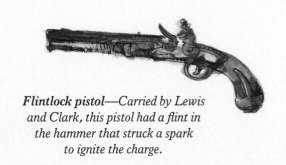

Flintlock pistol—*Carried by Lewis and Clark, this pistol had a flint in the hammer that struck a spark to ignite the charge.*

Mountain Man Lingo

cache—hidden goods, often plews (beaver skins), carefully wrapped and buried

coup—a blow or a touch given to an enemy in battle. Among American Indians, this was an act of bravery.

didin's—food

fat cow—high-living

foofaraw—fancy fixin's

good didin's—buffalo-bone-marrow soup, ribs and raw buffalo liver. Roasted beaver tail was the mountain men's favorite good didin's.

go under—die

hos—person

poor bull—hard life; see *what Joe Meek ate**

porkeater—a greenhorn or tenderfoot, specifically someone who hadn't gotten used to eating whatever was at hand, most often hominy (a form of corn) cooked in grease

tangle root—rotgut whiskey drunk by keelboatmen; said to be the only cure for hoop-snake bite

**what Joe Meek ate*—the food of the hard life: crisped soles of moccasins, boiled-up large black crickets and ants fresh from an anthill. Joe Meek stuck his hand deep into an anthill and licked the ants off his hands.

Bibliography

Botkin, B. A. *A Treasury of American Folklore.* New York: Crown, 1944.

Emrich, Duncan. *Folklore on the American Land.* Boston: Little, Brown, 1996.

Gilbert, Bil. *The Trailblazers.* Alexandria, Virginia: Time Life Books, 1973.

Knowles, Thomas, ed. *The West That Was.* New York: Wings Books, 1993.

Neider, Charles, ed. *The Great West.* New York: Bonanza Books, 1958.

Place, Marian T. *Beckwourth.* New York: Macmillan; London: Cromwell-Collier Press, Collier-Macmillan Limited, 1970.

Reader's Digest. *American Folklore and Legend.* Pleasantville, New York: Reader's Digest Association, 1978.

Richardson, Albert D. *Beyond the Mississippi.* Hartford, Connecticut: American Publishing Company, 1867.

Rounds, Glen, ed. *Mountain Men: George Frederick Ruxton's Firsthand Accounts of Fur Trappers and Indians in the Rockies.* New York: Holiday House, 1966.

Shepard, Betty, ed. *Mountain Man, Indian Chief: The Life and Adventures of Jim Beckwourth.* New York: Harcourt, Brace & World, 1968.

Ward, Geoffrey. *The West: An Illustrated History.* Boston: Little, Brown, 1996.

Author's Note

The mountain men were fortune hunters of less than tender sensibilities. Certainly they were unsympathetic to the animals they trapped nearly to extinction. As trailblazers and storytellers they inspired adventurous pioneers to brave the brutal odds and settle the Western wilderness. Their tales also inspired Americans with no inclination to leave their crowded Eastern cities or quiet farms to imagine that they, like free trappers, were the equal of anyone. I've tried to be true to the spirit of the tales. If I adjusted a few particulars, just remember what Ol' Black Harris said:

"Scalp my old head, marm," sez he with a wink,

"if'n all I claim ain't true, then I aren't a mountain man!"

———❖———

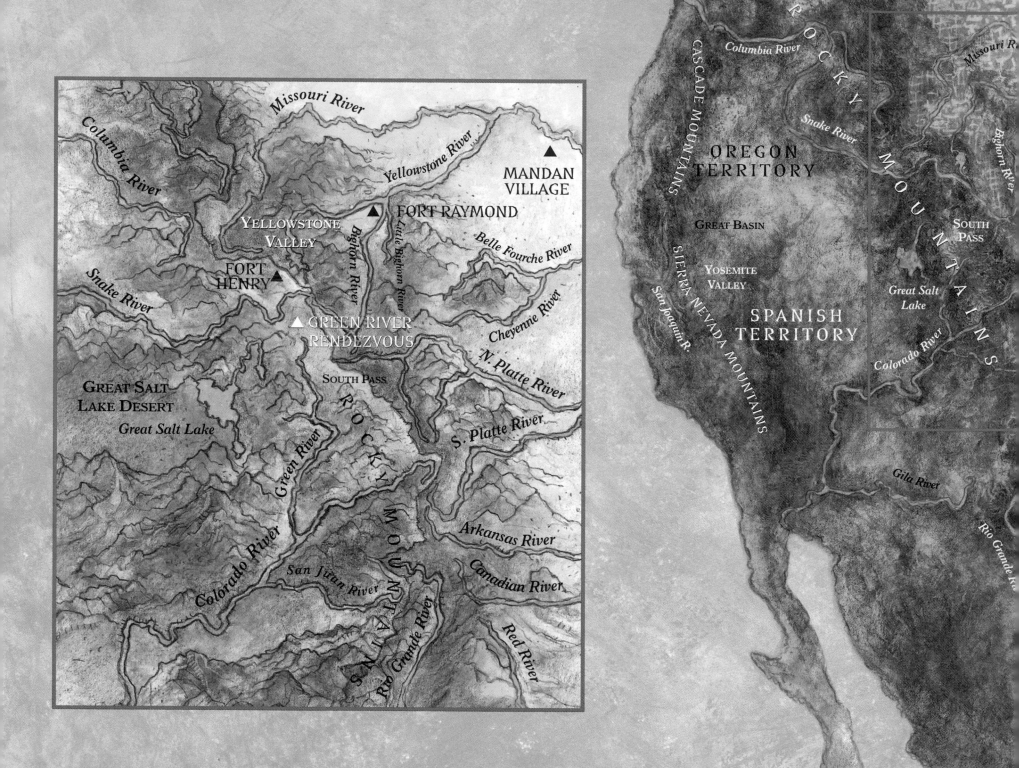